Me and My Animal Friends

to Beatrice ♡ Ralph

Ralph Covert

illustrated by Laurie Keller

Christy Ottaviano Books
Henry Holt and Company
New York

Elephants
and antelopes
and kangaroos,
wallabies
and penguins
from the zoo.

DING DONG!

WELCOME

Snakes
and
squirrels
and
little
brown
bats,
acrobatic
circus
cats.

Blue fish, red fish,
galloping goats,
puffins and camels
and piranhas in moats.

Dinosaur babies
and cows
and pigs

and
a
horse
as
small
as
a
dog
is
big.

And I wish, I really wish,
I really, really wish
they could be my pets.
Oh, please, pretty please,
from the bottom
of my heart
to the top of my head.

I'll be good, really good,
I'll be really,
REALLY GOOD
and you know I would
feed 'em all
every day
and at night I'd
tuck 'em all
in their beds.

NOooooooo

6 celots
and
lots
of
sloths
and
fleas,

a great horned owl and a chimpanzee.

A gecko
and a
goose
and a
humpback
whale,

Yeeeha!

a Minnesota minnow
and a South Dakota snail.

A

tiger that
can hop
on just
one leg,
seventeen
chipmunks
doing a jig.

An anteater, parakeet, a dolphin, frog,

and a BIG as small as a HORSE is DOG.

And I wish,
I really wish,
I REALLY,

REALLY
WISH

they could be my pets.

Oh, PLease,
Pretty please,

from the bottom
of my heart to the top of my head.

I'll be good, really good,
I'll be **really, really good**

and you know I would
feed 'em all every day

and at night
I'd tuck 'em all
in their beds.

Jumping
and
bouncing
and
climbing
in
trees,

swimming to the bottom of the deep blue sea.

Tunnel with the ants,
buzz with a bee,
ride a unicorn unicycle
up in a tree.

And if you say

NO

to that,
how about maybe
a **dog**
→
or a **cat?**
←

And I wish, I really wish,

I REALLY,

REALLY WISh

they could be my pets.

oh, PLe

ase pretty please,
from the bottom
of my heart
to the top of my head.
I'll be good, REALLY GOOD,
I'll be
really,
REALLY GOOD
and you know I would
feed 'em all, every day
and at night I'd
tuck 'em all in their beds.

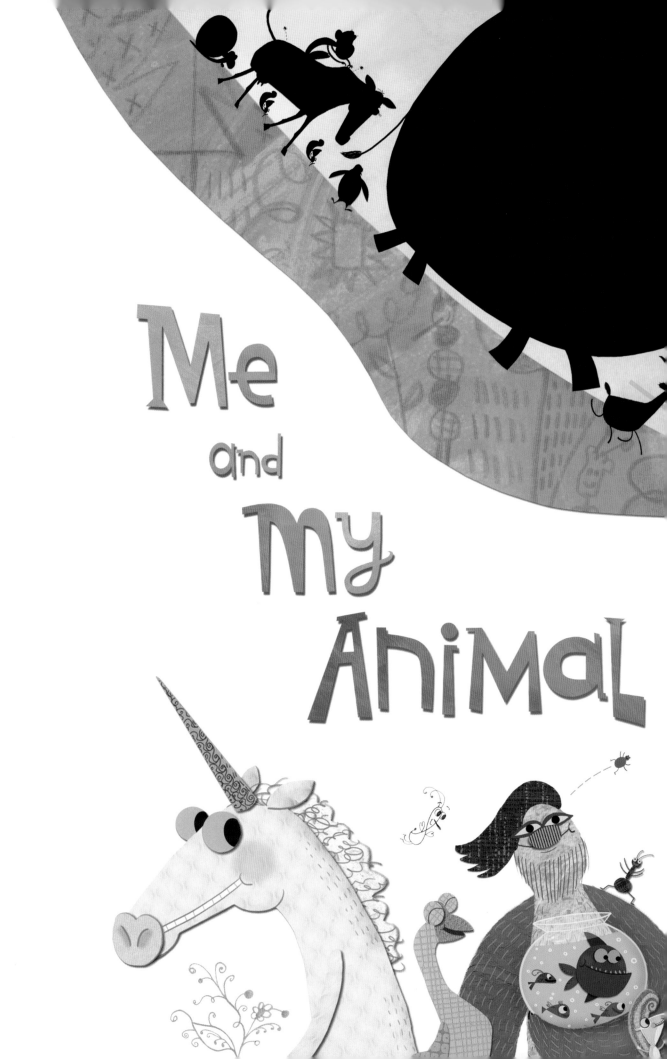

Me and My Animal

FrieNds!

Come play along with Ralph

Animal Friends (Ralph Covert / Waterdog Music / ASCAP)

C#m
Elephants and antelopes and kangaroos,

Em
Wallabies and penguins from the zoo.

C#m
Snakes and squirrels and little brown bats,

Em
Acrobatic circus cats.

C#m
Blue fish, red fish, galloping goats,

Em
Puffins and camels and piranhas in moats.

C#m
Dinosaur babies and cows and pigs,

Em
And a horse as small as a dog is big.

D   D/C#   G/B
And I wish, I really wish / I really, really wish

     Am   G   D/F
They could be my pets / Oh please, pretty please,

        Em   A
From the bottom of my heart to the top of my head,

D   D/C#   G/B
I'll be good, really good, I'll be really really good

      Am   G
and you know I would feed 'em all, every day

D/F#   Em   A
And at night I'd tuck 'em all in their beds.

C#m
Ocelots and lots of sloths and fleas,

      Em
A great horned owl and a chimpanzee.

C#m
A gecko and a goose and a humpback whale,

Em
A Minnesota minnow and a South Dakota snail.

C#m
A tiger that can hop on just one leg,

     Em
Seventeen chipmunks doing a jig.

C#m
An anteater, parakeet, dolphin frog,

     Em
And a big as small as a horse is dog.

D   D/C#   G/B
And I wish, I really wish / I really, really wish

     Am   G   D/F
They could be my pets / Oh, please, pretty please,

       Em
From the bottom of my heart to the top of my head.

      A
I'll be good, really good, I'll be really, really good

D   D/C#   G/B
and you know I would feed 'em all, every day

Am   G
And at night I'd tuck 'em all in their beds.

D/F#   Em   A

G   A   D
Me and my animal friends!

Amaj7   A7   D   E
To sleep, we'll sleep, all my animal friends and me

Amaj7   A7
And we'll dream, oh, we'll dream

    D   E
Of all the things we'll do tomorrow.

C#m
Jumping and bouncing and climbing in trees,

    Em
Swimming to the bottom of the deep blue sea.

C#m
Tunnel with the ants, buzz with a bee,

   Em
Ride a unicorn unicycle up in a tree.

C#m
And if you say "NO" to that,

   Em
How 'bout maybe a dog or a cat?

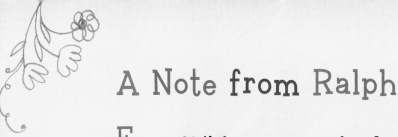

A Note from Ralph

For my birthday one year when I was a kid, we visited the zoo. My parents had recently hinted that I could have any pet I wanted, and as I looked around at all the different animals, my heart raced with excitement at the possibilities.

Ocelots, zebras, crocodiles, and kangaroos . . . which of these marvelous beasts would I choose for my pet? I made list after list over the next few weeks and gradually began lobbing out suggestions. To my surprise, my mom and dad weren't open to the possibility that having an elephant at our house would be pretty awesome. A penguin, maybe? A giraffe? A monkey? No, no, and no. Hmmm . . . they finally agreed I could have a puppy, but the question still tickles my imagination: if you could have ANY animal for a pet, which one would YOU choose?

*To Coffee (Cattie Coocoo), an animal
friend who will be missed*

—R. C.

*For all my fellow animal lovers in the
world and for Rilynne, who loves
"the dancing man" (Ralph)*

—L. K.

Henry Holt and Company, LLC
Publishers since 1866
175 Fifth Avenue
New York, New York 10010
www.HenryHoltKids.com

Henry Holt® is a registered trademark of Henry Holt and Company, LLC.
Text copyright © 2009 by Ralph Covert
Illustrations copyright © 2009 by Laurie Keller
"Me and My Animal Friends" lyrics and music copyright © Waterdog Music (ASCAP)
Photographs of Ralph Covert on jacket, title page, and Note from Ralph page
© Peter Thompson, © Waterdog music

Library of Congress Cataloging-in-Publication Data
Covert, Ralph.
Me and my animal friends / words and music by Ralph Covert;
illustrations by Laurie Keller. — 1st ed.
p.   cm.
"Christy Ottaviano Books."
Summary: Two children venture across land and sea looking at everything
from elephants to ants, promising that they will be very good and
take care of them if only they can have them as pets. Includes music.
ISBN-13: 978-0-8050-8736-9 / ISBN-10: 0-8050-8736-2
1. Children's songs, English—United States—Texts. 2. Animals—Songs and music—Texts.
[1. Songs. 2. Animals—Songs and music. 3. Pets—Songs and music.] I. Keller, Laurie, ill.
II. Ralph's World (Musical group). III. Title.
PZ8.3.C8336Me 2009   784.42—dc22   [E]   2008038223

First edition—2009
Printed in March 2009 in China by South China Printing Company Ltd.,
Dongguan City, Guangdong Province, on acid-free paper. ∞

The illustrations for this book were created using acrylic paint and collage on
Arches watercolor paper and assembled in Photoshop on a Macintosh computer.

1 3 5 7 9 10 8 6 4 2